WORLD CUP HEROES

WORLD CUP HEROES

David Bedford

Illustrated by Keith Brumpton

www.littleharebooks.com

Little Hare Books
an imprint of
Hardie Grant Egmont
85 High Street
Prahran, Victoria 3181, Australia

www.littleharebooks.com

Illustrations by Keith Brumpton and Xou Creative, 2010

First published 2010

National Library of Australia
Cataloguing-in-Publication entry

Bedford, David, 1969-

World cup heroes / David Bedford; illustrator, Keith Brumpton.

978 1 921541 29 2 (pbk.)

Bedford, David, 1969- Team; 9.

For primary school age.

Soccer stories.

Brumpton, Keith.

823.92

Cover design by Xou Creative (www.xou.com.au)
Set in 13.5/21 pt Giovanni by Clinton Ellicott
Printed through Polskabooks
Printed at Rzeszow Zaklady Graficzne, Rzeszow, Poland, April 2010

5 4 3 2 1

For Keith Brumpton—big thanks

DB

Prof Gertie | Darren | Harvey | Rita | Matt | Steffi | Mark 1

Chapter 1

The Team needed a goal. Harvey had to score.

He placed the ball down carefully, nestling it onto the grass. It was the last match of the season. The Team were drawing nil–nil with the Wild Cats. And the Wild Cats were a point ahead of The Team at the top of the league.

The Team had to win this game to become league champions. But time had almost run out. Harvey's free kick on the edge of the Wild Cats penalty area would be the last action of the game.

Harvey took six paces back, then looked up.

The Wild Cats had made a wall so tall and wide that Harvey couldn't see through to the goal.

Harvey put his hands on his hips.

I know where the goal is, he told himself. And I know what I have to do.

With a short run-up, Harvey struck through the ball.

THOCK!

Ten paces in front of him, the players in the Wild Cats wall jumped. The ball skimmed over their heads, still rising. The shot looked too high.

Then the ball began to dip.

As the wall broke up, Harvey saw the Wild Cats goalkeeper dive.

But he was too late. The net billowed as the ball hit it. The referee blew her whistle once for a goal, then three more times to signal the end of the game. The Team erupted in a terrific cheer. They had just won the league title for the second year running.

The Team huddled together. "I don't believe it!" said Rita ecstatically. "We used to be *so* rubbish!"

Harvey remembered The Team's first season, when they lost every game for months.

"Steffi was worse than useless in the beginning," said Matt.

"And I was still better than you!" snorted Steffi.

"We *never* scored," said Darren, "and our defence leaked goals like a sieve!"

"And now we're the best team around," said Rita. "All thanks to our fabulous supporters."

Harvey followed Rita's gaze to where The Team's number-one fan, Professor Gertie, was doing a victory dance along the sideline. She was partnered by her greatest invention, the football-playing robot, Mark 1. Even though his head was made from a rubbish bin, Mark 1 had a genius football brain and formidable football skills. The robot had used his talents to train The Team, and now The Team's hard work had paid off.

"Our dreams have come true," said Rita. "Right, Harvey?"

Harvey was about to agree, but hesitated. "Well ..." he said. "Some of them have."

"Do you have another dream?" asked Darren. "Is there something else we can win?"

Harvey felt himself blushing. "The World Cup," he said quietly. He was sure The Team would laugh. To his surprise, he saw a faraway look come into their eyes.

"In my World Cup dream," said Rita softly, "I score a last-minute penalty against the best keeper in the world."

"I *save* a last-minute penalty," said Darren, miming tipping a ball over the crossbar with his fingertips. "Howzat!"

"I'm Man of the Match," said Matt confidently, puffing out his chest with pride.

"And I'm Face of the Finals," said Steffi, fluttering her eyelashes.

"There isn't a Face of the Finals!" spluttered Matt.

"Yes, there is," insisted Steffi. "The Face of the Finals is the player the fans love the most."

"It's World Cup fever," said Darren. "We've all got it."

The World Cup finals were starting in just a few days' time. What was more, their home country was hosting the games. The Team had been looking forward to the World Cup for

months. Harvey should have guessed he hadn't been the only one dreaming about it.

"Is your dream like ours, Harvey?" wondered Rita.

Harvey looked around at his team mates. As he did so, his own World Cup dream popped into his mind. The Team were standing on the pitch in a huge stadium, which was filled with supporters waving banners and making a deafening noise. An announcer was calling out their names through a loudspeaker … "Darren — goalkeeper! … Rita — attacker! …"

"In my dream," Harvey told his team mates, "*The Team* are playing. All of us."

Harvey saw his team mates' faces light up as they imagined the scene.

Steffi, though, shook her head. "You're not a bad player, Harv," she said. "And we're a pretty good team. But we're not *world class*."

"How do you know?" said Matt. "We might be."

"Even if we were," said Steffi, "there's no way The Team could play together. Countries choose players from all different teams to represent them in the World Cup. And they're hardly going to pick juniors."

Darren rounded on Steffi. "It's Harvey's dream, okay? You don't have to spoil it."

"Just because Harvey has a dream," Steffi replied stubbornly, "it doesn't mean it's really going to happen."

Harvey didn't argue. Lots of his dreams for The Team had come true. They'd won gold and silver medals. They'd also won the Pyramid Cup, and they held the Superstars Record. But Harvey knew his World Cup dream wasn't likely to come true.

Just then, Professor Gertie and Mark 1 skipped towards them, and Harvey and his team mates joined in their celebration dance. The Team had achieved more than most teams ever did. It was time to enjoy their success, and forget about impossible dreams.

That night, though, Harvey dreamed about the World Cup again. This time, The Team were playing in the final. And they were winning.

Chapter 2

Harvey woke up earlier than he'd planned to on Monday morning. It was the first day of the holidays, and he was hoping to rest after a busy school term.

CREEAAK!

Harvey knew what made that sound. It was the door to Professor Gertie's inventing tower. Harvey stood up on his bed and peered out of his window. Professor Gertie was walking down Baker Street. She was wearing a jacket and skirt, and she carried a shiny briefcase.

Harvey scratched his head. Professor Gertie didn't usually leave her tower in the morning, when her inventing brain worked best. And Harvey had *never* seen her dressed so smartly.

Mark 1 stepped from the tower, closed the door, and marched after Professor Gertie.

Harvey rubbed his eyes. Mark 1 was wearing a brown suit and tie. The last time he'd worn that outfit was when he'd been the

Teacher Machine and taught Harvey to pass a school test.

Harvey didn't have a clue what his neighbours were up to, but he wasn't surprised when Darren and Rita, who were racing up the hill on their bikes, didn't even recognise them.

Darren looked up, spotted Harvey at his window, and bellowed excitedly, "Harvey! It's the World Cup. *We're playing!*"

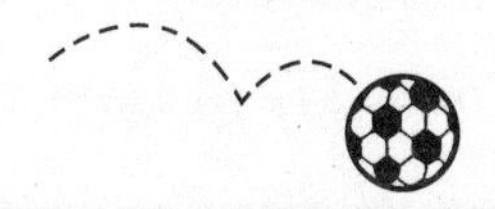

Harvey let Darren and Rita into his house. They were both red-cheeked and breathing heavily.

Rita handed Harvey a letter. "This was delivered to my house an hour ago," she said.

Harvey sat down on his sofa with the letter. It was a single sheet of silver paper. On the back there was a symbol like a soccer ball streaking across the page, and three words:

World Cup Heroes

Harvey didn't know what that meant. He flipped over the letter and read:

Dear The Team,

Congratulations! You have been chosen, as champions of your local league, to compete in **World Cup Heroes***.*

World Cup Heroes *is a tournament designed to test teamwork, courage and skill.*

The tournament takes place at the Majestic Stadium this Wednesday at 6pm.

The winners of **World Cup Heroes** *will watch the opening ceremony of the World Cup finals from the best seats in the country!*

See you soon,

Cassius

Harvey traced the signature with his finger, his whole body tingling. Cassius was famous for scoring the greatest goal of all time. He had fired an unstoppable shot from the centre spot, straight after kick-off. Just meeting Cassius would be a dream come true for Harvey.

"How do we get to the stadium?" said Harvey. "It's a long way."

"My dad said he'd take us in his bus," said Rita.

"Your dream is coming true, Harv," said Darren, hugging himself. "The Team are going to play a match in a World Cup tournament!"

Rita frowned. "The letter doesn't say we're playing an actual *match*," she said.

"What else could we be doing?" said Darren. "It's a tournament, isn't it?"

Rita shrugged. "I suppose," she said. Then she smiled. "I just can't believe we're going to be in a World Cup event!"

"Well, we are," said Darren. He held up his hands, and Rita and Harvey clapped them.

Harvey, Darren and Rita spent the day letting their team mates know they were going to a World Cup tournament. Matt nearly fainted. Steffi screamed, then booked an appointment with her hairdresser for that afternoon.

The last people to tell were Professor Gertie and Mark 1. As Harvey arrived home at the end of the day, he saw them trudging up Baker Street. Harvey ran over to them and held up the letter so that they could both read it.

Mark 1's jaw dropped open with a clang. "Fan-taztic!" he said in his strange mechanical voice.

A look of wonder came over Professor Gertie's face. "We have to be ready for anything," she said eagerly, raising her hands in the air.

Harvey loved seeing her like this. He could almost imagine ideas going off in her brain like fireworks.

"The Team must give Maximum Effort!" she commanded. "And most importantly of all …"

And suddenly, she stopped. Her arms dropped weakly to her sides. "Oh," she said. "I forgot. Silly me."

"Are you all right?" said Harvey.

"I'm afraid I have some bad news," Professor Gertie said. "Mark 1 and I can't be part of The Team anymore. We are too busy for football."

"But — why?" said Harvey in amazement.

"Wee havv new jobz," said Mark 1, his head drooping. "Sorree, Harvee. Gamme ovverr."

Chapter 3

"I don't understand," said Harvey. "Have The Team done something wrong?"

"Definitely not," said Professor Gertie.

"So why can't you keep helping us with your inventions?" said Harvey.

"I can't invent anything else for The Team," said Professor Gertie, "because I am no longer an inventor." She pointed to a sign on her gate that read:

Inventing Tower ***Closed***

"It was always my dream to invent," she said. "Alas, it hasn't come true."

"It has!" said Harvey. "You've invented loads of things!"

"But all of them are worthless," said Professor Gertie.

"Mark 1 is not worthless," said Harvey firmly. "He's a football genius. And our teacher bought one of your Lock Jaw pencil cases for everyone in our class — they're brilliant!"

"Mark 1 is my greatest achievement," agreed Professor Gertie. "And my Lock Jaw is faultless. The problem is, the Lock Jaw is the only invention I have ever sold for more than a few pennies. And it did not make enough money to pay even one of my many, many bills."

She opened her briefcase with a *snip!* and took out a thick wad of envelopes. Harvey saw the words "Last Chance to Pay" stamped in red letters on the topmost one.

"I have bills for electricity, bills for gas, bills for chemicals, bills for batteries and bills for fire extinguishers. Inventing costs money, Harvey," she said sadly. "If I can't pay my bills, I will have to sell my inventing tower."

Harvey shook his head. He never imagined Professor Gertie doing anything but inventing in her tower, and helping The Team.

"I start my new job tomorrow," said Professor Gertie. "Mark 1 shall be my assistant."

"What about World Cup Heroes?" said Harvey. "You both have to be there!"

"Mark 1 and I would like nothing better than to cheer The Team on to their next success," said Professor Gertie. "But alas, we have to work late on Wednesdays."

And with that, Professor Gertie bustled inside the tower with Mark 1, leaving Harvey staring after her.

On Tuesday morning, Harvey left his house at a run. His football boots dangled from one shoulder. The Team had only one day to get ready for World Cup Heroes. They'd have to spend most of the following day getting to the stadium in time for the tournament. The Team had arranged to meet at their practice pitch as early as they could.

Harvey skidded to a stop. A shopping trolley full of junk was blocking his path.

A note attached to the trolley read:

Harvey!

Mark 1 wants you to have these, my last-ever inventions. They are untested, *but* might *help.*

Good luck!

Love, Professor G. xx

The trolley squeaked loudly as Harvey pushed it to the pitch, and he couldn't help wondering if the jumble of objects it contained would really help The Team. Professor Gertie's inventions didn't always work the way they were supposed to.

The Team were waiting for him on the pitch. "Is this stuff from Professor Gertie?" Matt asked curiously. "I knew we could rely on her!"

Harvey was about to explain that this was the last time Professor Gertie could help The Team, when someone barged into him. It was a girl wearing thick make-up, and hair shaped like a beehive.

"Er ... who are you?" said Harvey.

Matt snorted. "Don't worry, mate," he said. "Nobody else knew who she was either. You're looking at the Face of the Finals. Steffi is somewhere underneath, I think."

Steffi ignored Matt. She tugged out the nearest invention from the trolley, and set it down on the grass. It was a heavy box on wheels, with a long, bendy tube stuck on top.

Harvey knew exactly what it was, because he'd seen Professor Gertie using it. "It's the professor's homemade vacuum cleaner," he said.

"I'm not doing chores!" said Darren.

"I don't think it's used for cleaning anymore," said Rita. She pointed to the side of the box, where "Snake Ladder" had been spelled out in curving letters. Under it were the words "Reverse Thrust!" and "Battery time: 90 minutes max!". A large orange button was labelled, "ON/OFF".

Rita pressed the button warily with her boot. The box began to vibrate and screech like a jet engine. Harvey took a step back as the bendy tube straightened and stood up like a squashy-looking drainpipe. Dusty air blasted from the top of it.

"If it's a Snake Ladder," shouted Rita, "I guess we're supposed to climb it!" She jumped on to the tube, gripping it with her legs. To Harvey's surprise, she hung in the air.

Darren was impressed. "Keep climbing!" he hollered.

Rita pulled herself up easily. She waved at them from the top. "This is great!" she said. "I can see Professor Gertie's inventing tower from here!" She climbed down, grinning.

Darren went next. "Amazing!" he called down. "You have a go, Harv."

Harvey let everyone else take a turn first, before jumping on the Snake Ladder. He tried pulling himself up, but after several minutes he was only centimetres above the ground.

"Come on, mate!" encouraged Darren. "It's like climbing a thick rope. Anyone can do it!"

Harvey could have told Darren that climbing had never been his thing, but he felt embarrassed. He stepped off the Snake Ladder and pressed the orange button to turn it off.

"World Cup Heroes will be testing our *match* skills," he told his team mates. "We should be practising those."

Darren, though, was already lifting Professor Gertie's old ironing board from the shopping trolley. It had been freshly painted with a picture of a seal surfing a wave and playing a saxophone. "Bop Board" was printed in small letters along one edge, and there was a speaker taped to the front end.

Darren stood on the Bop Board — and suddenly it began to buck up and down. The speaker blared and the ironing board's legs beat out the rhythm on the ground.

Boom, badda, boom, badda, boom boom boom!

"Whoa!" cried Darren, twisting and bending as he tried to stay on the board. When he tumbled to the grass, The Team surged forwards to have a go. Steffi sang as she bopped. Matt stayed on for so long, in the end he jumped off to let someone else take a turn.

"This isn't football-related, either," said Harvey.

"It's fun, though!" cried Rita, as she was bucked off. "You have your turn, then we can try the next invention."

Harvey put one foot on the Bop Board — and was sent flying through the air.

"You gotta learn to bop, mate!" chuckled Darren. "Let's try the next invention!"

He lifted Harvey's old soccer ball from the trolley. The Team didn't play with it anymore because it had been burst by a splinter. Now, though, it looked like it had been cut in half and sewn back together again. "Scatterball" had been written around the middle of the ball in thick marker pen.

Matt shook the Scatterball. It made a jangling noise as if there were bells inside. "There's no button, or anything," he reported.

"Let's do some match training," advised Harvey. "We can't waste any more time." His stomach told him they'd already missed lunch.

"Good idea," said Matt. "We can train with this Scatterball!" He threw it high to Steffi, who stepped forward to control it on her chest.

Suddenly the Scatterball changed course, bouncing off Steffi's shoulder. "Hey!" she said.

Rita ran to where the Scatterball had fallen. She smiled mischievously, then flicked it towards The Team, calling, "Scatter!"

The Team dived out of the way.

Harvey, though, didn't see it coming. "Oof!" he said, as the Scatterball hit him in the stomach.

"Sorry!" said Rita.

"Professor Gertie is a genius!" exclaimed Darren. "She has made a ball *that changes direction in midair*!"

The Team kicked the Scatterball at each other, seeing who dodged it best.

Harvey was getting frustrated. "Professor Gertie's inventions are distracting us," he said. "We should be finetuning our match skills."

"There's only one more invention," said Rita. "We still have time to train." She bent over the trolley, then held up Professor Gertie's bicycle pump. "Wild Web — family fun" was scrawled along the barrel. Rita shook the pump. Harvey heard something inside sloshing about.

"I know what to do," said Matt. He took the pump from Rita, aimed it into the sky above them, and pumped.

SPLOTZ!

A rainbow-coloured jet of liquid shot from the end, rising straight up above The Team. As Harvey watched, the rainbow began to separate into long, brightly coloured strings that stuck to each other to make a tangled net.

And then the tangled net fell on The Team.

"Uh-oh," said Matt.

Harvey felt the Wild Web stick to his arms and legs. He tried to twist free, but couldn't. It was like being tied up in sticky elastic bands.

The Team struggled to unwrap themselves.

"It's impossible!" said Rita, whose hands were tangled in the Wild Web.

Darren tried to peel the Wild Web from his nose. "I have a bad feeling about this invention," he warned.

By the time The Team had escaped from the Wild Web, the moon was shining above them. Harvey sighed. The one day they had to prepare for World Cup Heroes was over, and The Team hadn't done any football training for the biggest challenge they would ever face.

Chapter 4

Early the next morning, Harvey watched Professor Gertie and Mark 1 leave the inventing tower together. They wore matching tracksuits. Mark 1 carried an enormous sack.

Harvey had no idea what they were doing, and he had no time to find out. A bus had just turned the corner into Baker Street, and Harvey was still in his pyjamas.

Fifteen minutes later, Harvey ran from his house and onto the bus. The Team cheered.

"Sorry, Mr Syal!" Harvey told Rita's dad, who had just beeped the bus's horn for the third time.

"No problem," smiled Rita's dad. "We don't want to be late, though!" He started the bus, and Harvey felt a burst of excitement. They were on their way to play in a World Cup tournament!

Harvey walked to the back seat, clapping hands with his team mates as he passed.

Everyone looked smart in their bright Team kits. They hadn't trained for the tournament as Harvey had hoped, but there was nothing they could do about that now.

Harvey sat down between Rita and Darren.

Darren frowned as the bus moved off. "Aren't Professor Gertie and Mark 1 coming with us?" he asked Harvey.

"No," Harvey replied. He told Rita and Darren about Professor Gertie's bills, and how she and the robot had taken new jobs.

Rita looked downcast. "I don't believe it," she said. "Professor Gertie should stick to inventing, because she's brilliant at it. And Mark 1 should train The Team, because that's what he was made for."

"What kind of job could a professor and a football machine find, anyway?" wondered Darren.

"I don't know," said Harvey simply.

Then the bus stopped at some traffic lights in the centre of town, and Harvey found himself staring at quite the oddest sight he'd ever seen.

Professor Gertie was standing on the high street, dressed as a giant football boot. Propped beside her was a sign that read: *BIG SALE at SPOYLE SPORTS.*

Mark 1 was standing next to Professor Gertie. He was holding a huge cardboard hand that pointed to Spoyle's sports shop behind them. Mark 1 also had a large inflatable football strapped to his head.

Professor Gertie lifted her Shouting Mask to her mouth. The mask was one of her first-ever inventions. It made her voice sound like a thousand fans, all roaring at once, and she regularly used it to cheer on The Team.

Next, Professor Gertie sounded out a drum-beat with her mouth, and Mark 1 began a robotic dance. Passers-by stopped to watch.

Harvey felt the bus tilt as The Team rushed to the window for a better look.

"Professor Gertie certainly knows how to grab people's attention," said Steffi.

"That robot," said Matt, "does the best robotic dance I have ever seen."

"Mark 1 doesn't look very happy, though," said Rita.

Suddenly, Professor Gertie looked up and saw Harvey. She gave him a thumbs up. Harvey, though, wasn't fooled. Even with her face almost covered by the Shouting Mask, he could tell that Professor Gertie looked sad and left out. Harvey wanted to yell and stop the bus, so that The Team's number-one fan, and her assistant, could join them. But it was too late. The lights changed and the bus moved on.

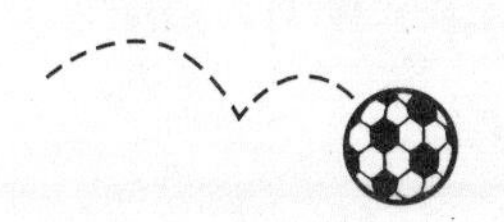

Later that afternoon, Harvey pressed his face against the bus window as the Majestic Stadium came into view. Harvey had never seen anything like it. The stadium was built like a fortress. Four giant-sized battlements were each topped with tall turrets, and each turret was flying a flag.

"Look at all the fans!" said Rita, pointing to the streams of people who were making their way towards the stadium. "Are they all here to watch us?"

Darren whistled. "This is going to be awesome," he said.

Harvey followed The Team off the bus. Once outside, he heard chanting rhythms all around him. Three girls with long, dark hair jostled past, waving green flags. Darren almost tripped over a man with a bare chest painted with blue stripes.

"There are fans from all around the world here!" said Steffi.

Harvey wished The Team's supporters were there, too. Professor Gertie and Mark 1 were missing out on The Team's biggest adventure yet.

"This way!" called Rita's dad. The Team followed him across a drawbridge, and through the gigantic castle gates.

The greatest goalscorer of all time was

waiting for them inside. Harvey's legs felt weak.

"The Team?" said Cassius, beaming. "Great! You are just in time. Follow me."

"Good luck!" Rita's dad called after them.

Cassius led The Team along a corridor until they came to two doors. One door was labelled, "Stadium". The other door was labelled, "Dungeon".

Cassius opened the "Dungeon" door.

"Er, sir," said Darren. "Aren't we going to the stadium?"

Cassius shook his head. "I am afraid not. The stadium will later tonight be hosting a ceremony to mark the start of the World Cup finals. Many international teams will be taking part. Their fans are already arriving."

"They're not our supporters, then?" said Darren disappointedly.

Cassius stopped by a door and held it open, revealing a brightly lit changing room. "Boot up as fast as you can," he said. "World Cup Heroes is about to begin!"

Harvey pushed off his trainers and fitted his boots. He tied his laces tightly, with fumbling fingers. His heart was racing. Even if World

Cup Heroes wasn't taking place in the main stadium, this was still the chance of a lifetime. The Team had to be ready to play the best football of their lives.

Cassius stood patiently by an unmarked door. He gripped the handle. "It is time," he said.

Rita caught Harvey's eye. She tried to grin, but her mouth twisted nervously. Darren was holding his breath. Matt looked lost. Steffi was trying to fluff up her hair, but she was making a mess of it.

Harvey turned to his team mates. He had to help them focus. "We're ready for this," he told them. "Whatever we find on the other side of that door, we'll do as well as we can. We're The Team, and that's what we do."

Cassius yanked open the door, and The Team followed him into darkness.

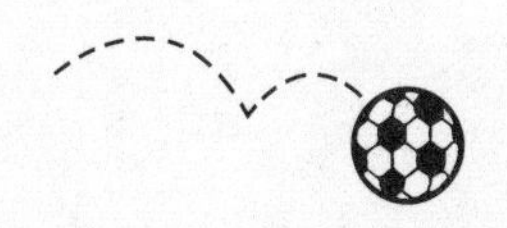

Harvey held his hand in front of his face, but he couldn't see it. He stopped walking.

Darren bumped into him from behind. "What's going on?" he hissed.

Cassius spoke. "You're in the Dungeon, a state-of-the-art training facility. The World Cup Heroes tournament will take place here."

Gradually, Harvey became aware that there were people standing beside The Team, shuffling their feet.

"The Team," said Cassius, "meet your opponents."

"Er, hello," said Harvey into the darkness.

A boy's voice spoke from right next to him. "We're the best."

Harvey sensed Darren bristle behind him. "We'll see about that," The Team's goalkeeper muttered.

"You don't understand," said the voice. "That's what our team is called: The Best."

Steffi giggled from Harvey's right-hand side. "You've *got* to be kidding," she said. "Who called you The Best?"

"We did," said the voice.

"Well, you'd better be good," Matt said, standing on Harvey's foot as he stepped forward. "Otherwise your name doesn't make sense."

"We have won every competition we've ever been in," replied the voice confidently. "That's why we're The Best."

The Team were stunned into silence.

Cassius spoke. "When the lights come on, you will all see an obstacle course ahead of you."

"An obstacle course?" said Harvey, thinking aloud. "Aren't we playing a match?"

"World Cup Heroes is designed to be the ultimate test of skill and courage," explained Cassius. "It is not an ordinary football game."

Harvey felt even more nervous. He'd been sure the tournament would feature a football match. Now he had no idea what to expect.

"Each team," said Cassius, "will find a ball the same colour as their shirts. The ball must be carried at all times. World Cup Heroes will be won by the team who shoots their ball *from*

no closer than the penalty spot into the goal at the end of the course. Teams may take as many shots as they need."

"Is there a goalkeeper?" asked Darren.

"No," said Cassius.

Darren sniffed, sounding unimpressed.

"I must warn you of some most important rules," said Cassius. "If any player falls from an obstacle, or drops the ball, they will have to begin the course again from the start. And *all* of a team's players must complete the obstacles before that team can shoot for goal."

Harvey's heart was now thumping in his chest. There were only two teams. The Team could win … if they did things right.

"GO!" said Cassius.

A siren sounded. Lights came on. Harvey squinted around. They were standing in the corner of an arena that housed a full-sized football pitch. There were tiers of seats on either side. About two dozen supporters dressed in yellow were watching expectantly.

They must be The Best supporters, thought Harvey.

An obstacle course stretched down the middle of the pitch towards the halfway line. Harvey spotted some kind of swimming pool, and some high walkways. And then Harvey's eyes were drawn to the first obstacle, and a feeling of dread rooted him to the spot.

It was the highest rope climb he had ever seen.

Chapter 5

The Best sprinted to the ropes. They were dressed entirely in yellow, and they were all taller than any player on The Team.

A black-haired girl with freckles picked up a yellow ball. "Captain!" she said, and handed the ball to a powerfully built boy with curly hair and blue eyes.

"I've got it," The Best captain replied confidently. Harvey recognised his voice. It was the same voice that had told them that The Best won everything they had ever tried to win.

The Best captain waited for one of his

team mates, a sporty-looking girl with glasses, to reach a platform at the top of the ropes. He tossed the ball to her, then began pulling himself up his own rope with ease.

The Team stared after The Best with wide eyes and open mouths.

And then Rita sprang forward. She scooped up The Team's red ball, stuffed it inside her shirt, and shinned up the nearest rope.

Then she raced past The Best captain, reached the high platform, and peered down. "What are you waiting for?" she yelled to her team mates. "*Climb!*"

The rest of The Team launched themselves at the ropes. Harvey gritted his teeth and pulled furiously. Why, he thought miserably, did the first obstacle have to be a rope climb? He'd never been good at ropes.

"Just concentrate on moving one hand over the other!" Rita called down helpfully.

Darren joined Rita on the platform. "Use your legs, mate!" he shouted to Harvey.

Harvey tried, but the rope slipped between his ankles. One of his boots touched the ground. He looked up at his team mates desperately. They were now all leaning over the edge of the high platform, looking concerned. There was no sign of The Best.

"I can't do it!" said Harvey. The Team were going to lose World Cup Heroes at the first obstacle, because their captain couldn't climb ropes. Harvey hung his head in despair.

Suddenly, the rope he was holding was nearly yanked out of his grasp. He began to rise quickly. The Team were pulling him up.

Then Matt and Steffi grabbed him under the arms and heaved him onto the platform.

"Th-thanks," said Harvey, out of breath.

"Just don't get any heavier," growled Steffi.

Harvey could see The Best's yellow shirts already far ahead. "Let's go," he said. The Team dashed after their opponents.

The platform led to a high walkway. The Best had already crossed the walkway, and had disappeared from view.

Harvey increased his speed. He reached the walkway ahead of his team mates — and was thrown to the floor as it buckled under him.

"It's a wobbly bridge!" warned Rita, from behind him.

Harvey knelt, but he couldn't stand up. He'd always been useless on wobbly bridges. This one was rocking him up, down and from side to side like a boat in a storm. Harvey began to feel sick.

"Are you hurt?" Steffi asked him.

"No," said Harvey. "I just can't balance."

"You need more practice on the Bop Board, mate," said Matt. "But for now … Steffi, you hold his legs."

"Wait —!" Harvey cried, as he was lifted and carried along swiftly by his team mates. The wobbly bridge undulated underneath him. Harvey felt like he was falling.

Steffi and Matt put him down on another high platform. Harvey stood up dizzily. The rest of The Team crossed the bridge easily.

"There are steps down from here," said Rita, jogging ahead. "We're not far behind The Best."

Harvey descended the steps behind Rita.

He watched their opponents on the next obstacle as he went. The Best were shuffling along wooden planks that zigzagged back and forth over a brightly lit swimming pool. As Harvey got nearer, he saw that the pool was filled with glittering plastic footballs.

Harvey led his team mates onto the first plank. The planks were wide enough to walk upon easily, even wearing football boots. And they didn't wobble.

Harvey increased his pace. The Best were only a few steps ahead.

"Why are they moving so slowly?" called Rita.

Harvey frowned. For some reason, The Best were all looking up at the roof. Harvey followed their gaze — and saw a row of cannons aimed at them.

BOOM!

Plastic footballs hurtled towards them.

"Scatterball!" yelled Matt, opening his legs wide enough for a ball to whizz between them. Harvey saw Steffi jerk her head sideways to stop a ball from hitting her on the chin. Rita skipped skilfully in the air as a ball skimmed under her knees. Darren ducked twice as two balls brushed the top of his hair.

Harvey watched The Best players crouching low and running as fast as they could.

And then a ball hit Harvey squarely in the face and he toppled backwards towards the ball pool below.

Chapter 6

Harvey felt two strong hands grab his shirt.

"I've got you!" Darren bellowed. "Now, somebody hold on to me!"

Harvey's boots were still on the plank, but he was leaning far back over the ball pool. For a moment he thought Darren would have to let go of him or else fall off the obstacle with him. But then Harvey felt himself being drawn back towards his team mates. He saw that Rita had hold of Darren by his collar. Matt held Rita's waist. Steffi was facing the cannons.

BOOM!

Another barrage of balls flew towards them. Steffi deflected them away with her body.

"I guess Scatterball wasn't Harvey's thing either," Matt commented as Harvey regained his balance and Darren let go of his shirt.

The Team began to move along the planks in a tight group, protecting their captain each time the cannons fired.

"I'm sorry," Harvey said, when The Team stepped safely back onto the grassy pitch.

"No worries," Rita said. "But we have to get after The Best!"

She pointed, and Harvey saw the yellow shirts of The Best players running down the pitch. For a moment Harvey thought they were heading straight for the goal. Then he realised there was one more obstacle for them to complete first: a net! It lay on the grass, stretching all the way to the centre circle. The front of the net was held up on sticks.

"They have to go under the net," said Harvey. "That should slow them down." And he tore after The Team's opponents.

If only, Harvey thought miserably, I was good at even one thing in the World Cup Heroes obstacle course!

He'd had to be pulled up the rope climb, carried across the wobbly bridge, and saved from being knocked into the ball pool. And now he was trapped under the net.

This time, The Team were unable to help him, because they were trapped, too. This net

wasn't sticky like Professor Gertie's Wild Web, but it weighed a ton. None of The Team had managed to scramble more than a few paces under it. They now lay pressed to the ground, barely able to move at all.

The Best players were ahead. Their greater strength was paying off as they crouched low and burrowed under the net like moles.

"We're finished," Harvey told his team mates. "We did as well as we could, but —"

He was cut off by a thunderous shout.

"**Keypp onnn, Harveee!**"

Harvey was so surprised, he choked. The strange, mechanical voice sounded exactly like Mark 1's. And to make that much noise, the robot had to be talking through Professor Gertie's Shouting Mask. Did that mean The Team's fans were here?

Harvey heard loud tutting and muttering sounds, followed by a voice saying, "**Give it to me — get off!**" And then another shout came, so loud it seemed to rock the arena's roof.

"Go, The Team!"

Darren lifted his head. "That's Professor Gertie!" he said.

Harvey tried to look towards the seats, but the net kept him pinned close to the ground and he couldn't see that far. Then chants of "**Keypp onnn, Harveee!**" and "**Go, The Team!**" began to resound around them.

Harvey felt a surge of pride. The Team's fans were unstoppable. They were there to support The Team through their most difficult times, no matter what.

Together, The Team players got to their knees. Then Harvey stood up. His whole body shook with effort as he supported the weight of the net with his shoulders. Without a word, Rita handed him their red ball.

The Team knew what to do. They all had to get through this one last obstacle. And then Harvey had to score to win the tournament.

"Let's do it for the fans," said Harvey.

The Team began to inch forward. Each player took it in turns to lift the net while their team mates crawled underneath it.

"**Keypp onnn, Harveee!**" Mark 1 yelled in encouragement.

Then, when Harvey came level with The Best captain, The Team moved into the lead for the first time in the tournament.

The Team crawled from under the net, with The Best close behind them. There was no time to lose. The Team darted forwards, towards the final obstacle.

Then Rita gasped. "Our ball!" she said. "Where is it?"

Harvey and The Team skidded to a halt, and The Best raced past them towards the open goal.

Chapter 7

Harvey spotted The Team's ball lying back in the middle of the net. Somehow, he had dropped it. His legs buckled. He sat down and put his head in his hands. It was the worst moment of his life.

The Team stood around him. Steffi broke the silence. "Harvey has to do the course again," she said weakly. "Otherwise we can't even take a shot at goal."

"That's the rule," whispered Matt.

Harvey could barely speak. He'd never thought he'd let The Team down so badly.

"I can't do the obstacles on my own," he said.

"You don't have to," Rita said. Her eyes were twinkling. "The rule is that if anyone loses the ball they have to complete the course from the start," she said. "It doesn't say your team can't help you, Harvey."

Harvey saw The Best captain reach the penalty spot and place his yellow ball down carefully. In seconds he would take a shot.

Suddenly Darren whooped with joy. *"Look at that goal!"*

Harvey felt his heart leap. The goal was tiny.

The goal mouth was no bigger than that of a basketball net. It would take a top shot to score, even from close range. The Team might still have a chance.

Harvey got to his feet just as The Best captain fired off a shot — and missed the goal. The Best fans groaned.

Matt bounded back over to the net obstacle, retrieved the red ball, and put it in Harvey's hands.

Harvey looked around his tired team mates. "Are you ready to do the whole course again?" he asked.

Without a word, The Team turned and raced back along the pitch to the rope climb. Harvey's whole body hurt, but he had the red ball in his hands — and The Team weren't beaten yet.

Harvey held the ball tightly as The Team pulled him up the rope.

"Go, The Team!"

He shoved it inside his shirt as The Team

carried him across the wobbly bridge. The Best fans groaned again, and Harvey guessed that their captain had missed another shot.

"Keypp onnn, Harveee!"

Harvey's team mates protected him from the cannons as he carefully shielded the ball.

"GO! GO! GO! GO! GO!"

The Team reached the net obstacle for the second time.

"We'll lift the net," Rita told Harvey. "You're going to need your strength on the other side."

His team mates held the net high as Harvey scrambled through. He heard The Best fans screaming urgently.

They must have missed again, Harvey thought. He might still have time.

Harvey crawled from the net and stood up in the centre circle. He tossed The Team's red ball in front of him. It rolled across the grass and stopped dead on the centre spot.

The Best captain took another shot from the penalty spot, rolling the ball slowly towards the goal with the side of his foot.

Harvey drew in a breath. This time, The Best's yellow ball was heading for the middle of the tiny goal.

The Best fans stood up. The Best players raised their arms.

Harvey sensed that all his team mates were standing around him, free of the net.

"Harvey," Darren breathed heavily, "it's now or never, mate!"

"**Shoooooot!**" urged Mark 1 from the crowd.

Harvey took two steps towards the red ball and struck it for all he was worth.

Chapter 8

Cassius led The Team along a corridor, through a tunnel, and on to the pitch of the Majestic Stadium. Ninety thousand spectators got to their feet and clapped.

High above them there was a giant-sized screen. On it, Harvey saw himself, smiling. There was a red ball tucked under his arm.

Cassius held up a microphone and said, "All cheer Harvey Boots — The Team Captain!"

There was thunderous applause. Then the stadium grew quiet as the screen replayed the last moments of World Cup Heroes.

Harvey watched himself crawl from the net and clamber to his feet. He seemed to wait an age before the rest of The Team joined him. Darren spoke. And then Harvey stepped towards the ball and fired it from the centre spot. The Team's red ball slammed into the tiny goal a split second before The Best's yellow ball crossed the goal line.

The crowd in the Majestic Stadium erupted once more in deafening cheers. Cassius clasped Harvey's hands. "That was some shot," he said. "*World class,*" he added seriously.

The screen showed Harvey and his team mates shaking hands with The Best, and then The Team were led from the Dungeon by Cassius. Harvey remembered Cassius telling him that the spectators in the stadium had been watching the World Cup Heroes tournament all along on the giant video screen.

Then The Team's faces appeared one by one on the screen as Cassius announced their names.

"Rita Syal — artful attacker!"

"Darren Riley — genius goalkeeper!"

"Matt Bartelski — demon defender!"

Finally, Steffi appeared on the screen. "Stefanie Bush — all round soccer superstar. And *Face of The Team*!"

Steffi struck a pose as cameras flashed.

Next, the screen showed two fans sitting in the crowd. One of them was still dressed as a football boot. Mr Syal was beside them. "And

here are The Team's fans," announced Cassius. "Professor Gertie Gallop, and Mark 1 Gallop!"

Professor Gertie waved madly. Then she climbed from her seat and waddled across to join The Team, dragging Mark 1 with her.

"We couldn't let The Team battle it out alone!" she said. "Our unique services were needed here — so we quickly packed in our jobs, and Mark 1 hitched us a lift."

"Your cheers were brilliant!" said Rita. "We needed our fans more than anything. And playing with your inventions turned out to be perfect practice for World Cup Heroes."

"What about paying your bills?" said Harvey. "If you don't keep your jobs, will you have to sell your inventing tower?"

"Oh, something will come up," said Professor Gertie. She sounded confident, but Harvey could tell she was putting it on so she didn't spoil The Team's big moment.

"Supporting The Team is just too important," Professor Gertie added, "especially now we're in the World Cup."

"Er," said Harvey. "We're not actually in the World Cup, Professor. Our prize for winning World Cup Heroes is a seat each at the opening ceremony later tonight."

Cassius, who was standing nearby, strode forward. "I have a surprise for you, Harvey," he said. The Team gathered around. "World Cup Heroes is only the beginning," said Cassius. "It is the first of many tournaments happening around the world."

"There will be lots of Heroes winners like us?" asked Rita.

"There will be one winning team from each country," said Cassius. "And, next year, they will all come together to play matches in a *Junior World Cup football tournament*!"

Harvey felt shivers rising up from his boots. "We're going to play in a World Cup?" he said.

"The Team will be representing your country!" said Cassius.

"It's your dream, Harvey," Steffi said. "It's come true. For all of us."

"There is just one problem," said Cassius, frowning. "We need someone to create new obstacles for future Heroes tournaments. It will not be easy to find a person of great enthusiasm, ability and invention."

"I can help you there," said Harvey, grinning. "Cassius, meet Professor Gertie. She is the greatest inventor ever. She won't let you down. And her assistant is a football genius."

Professor Gertie's eyes glinted. "Mark 1 and I can only work part time," she warned Cassius, "because it's important we support The Team as they take on the world."

Cassius bowed to Professor Gertie and Mark 1. "That will be perfect. I welcome you both to your new jobs," he said.

Mark 1 gave Cassius a hug.

Suddenly, a ball flew towards Harvey. He trapped it at his feet and noticed that several World Cup teams were warming up around him.

Harvey returned the ball to a nearby football superstar, but he tapped it back to Harvey. Harvey flicked it on to Rita, who sidefooted to Darren, who backheeled to Steffi.

"We're having a kickabout in the World

Cup!" laughed Rita. The rest of The Team began laughing, too. Harvey felt like he was walking on air. His friends had achieved so much by working hard and sticking together. And soon they would be playing teams from across the world, with the best fans they could wish for by their side.

"What about *after* the Junior World Cup?" said Darren. "Have you got more dreams, Harvey?"

"Lots," Harvey promised, looking around at his team mates. "And they're for each and every one of us."

David Bedford was born in Devon, in the south-west of England in 1969.

David wasn't always a writer. First he was a football player. He played for two teams: Appleton FC and Sankey Rangers. Although these weren't the worst teams in the league, they never won anything!

After school, David went to university and became a scientist. His first job was in America, where he worked on discovering new antibiotics.

David has always loved to read and decided to start writing stories himself. After a while, he left his job as a scientist and began writing full time. His novels and picture books have been translated into many languages around the world.

David lives with his wife and two children in Norfolk, England.

www.davidbedford.co.uk

Titles in The Team series

The Football Machine

Top of the League

Soccer Camp

Superteam

Banned!

Masters of Soccer

Football Rules

Soccer Superstars

World Cup Heroes